Polzunkov

*Dignity in Disgrace, The Mask of
Laughter,
and the Pain of Being Overlooked*

A Modern Translation

Adapted for the Contemporary Reader

Fyodor Dostoevsky

Translated by Tim Zengerink

Table of Contents

Preface - Message to the Reader

What If You Could Help Rebuild the Greatest Library in Human History?

Thousands of years ago, the Library of Alexandria stood as the crown jewel of human achievement — a sanctuary where the collected wisdom of every known civilization was gathered, preserved, and shared freely.

And then, it was lost.

Through fire, conquest, and the slow erosion of time, humanity lost not just books — but ideas, dreams, discoveries, and stories that could have changed the world forever.

Today, the Library of Alexandria lives again — and you are invited to be a part of its restoration.

Our mission is simple yet profound:

To rebuild the greatest library the world has ever known, and to translate all timeless works into every language and dialect, so that no seeker of knowledge is ever left behind again.

By joining our movement to rebuild the modern Library of Alexandria, you become part of an unprecedented mission:

Unlimited Access to the Greatest Audiobooks & eBooks Ever Written:

Instantly explore thousands of legendary works—Plato, Shakespeare, Jane Austen, Leo Tolstoy, and countless more. All instantly available to read or listen, placing a complete literary universe at your fingertips.

Beautiful Paperback & Deluxe Editions at Printing Cost

Own any title as an elegant paperback, deluxe hardcover, or stunning collectible boxset—offered to you at true printing cost, delivered straight to your door. Build your personal Library of Alexandria, crafted for beauty, built for durability, and worthy of proud display.

Fresh Translations for Modern Readers—in Every Language & Dialect

Enjoy timeless masterpieces reimagined in clear, contemporary language—no more outdated phrases or obscure references. Alongside the original versions, we're tirelessly translating these classics into every language and dialect imaginable, ensuring accessibility and understanding across cultures and generations.

Join a Global Renaissance of Literature & Knowledge

You directly support expanding our library, publishing deluxe editions at true cost, translating works into all global languages, and bringing humanity's greatest stories to people everywhere. By joining today, you're not just preserving a legacy of masterpieces; you set in motion a powerful wave of literary accessibility.

Become a Torchbearer of Knowledge.

Join us for free now at **LibraryofAlexandria.com**

Together, we will ensure that the light of human wisdom never fades again.

With gratitude and a shared love of knowledge,

The Modern Library of Alexandria Team

Visit:

www.libraryofalexandria.com

Or scan the code below:

Introduction

The Tragic Comedy of Social Invisibility and Internal Dignity

Fyodor Dostoevsky's early short story Polzunkov, published in 1848, is a compact but emotionally layered exploration of humiliation, social hierarchy, and the fragile search for dignity in a world that finds its entertainment in mockery. Often classified as one of his "lesser-known" works, Polzunkov nonetheless contains many of the psychological insights, character dynamics, and tonal complexities that would later define Dostoevsky's greatest novels. With equal parts satire and sorrow, Dostoevsky dissects the mechanisms of social exclusion and the quiet suffering endured by those dismissed as laughable or insignificant.

The story centers on a small, awkward, and eccentric clerk named Polzunkov, who has become the butt of jokes in his office. Laughed at for his clumsy appearance and erratic speech, he is tolerated at best and ridiculed at worst by his peers and superiors. During a party hosted by his employer, Polzunkov is invited for the express purpose of being laughed at—an object of entertainment rather than a guest. Yet beneath this surface of farce, Dostoevsky paints a moving portrait of a man with inner depth, quiet pride, and a deeply human longing to be respected, even loved.

As the story unfolds, we are drawn into the interior world of Polzunkov—his thoughts, his insecurities, and his quiet resolve. His attempt to maintain self-respect in the face of public degradation transforms the narrative from a comedic sketch into a tragic study of isolation. In Dostoevsky's hands, Polzunkov is not a caricature but a mirror: a reflection of the many individuals who, though dismissed as ridiculous or weak, possess a dignity unseen by those who judge them.

Polzunkov is not merely about cruelty; it is about the human spirit's resistance to cruelty. It is about what it means to live under the gaze of mockery and to survive with one's self-respect intact. This introduction delves into the narrative's themes of shame, social status, hidden virtue, and the painful dissonance between outward perception and inner reality.

A Man Made to Be Laughed At:
The Cost of Social Comedy

At first glance, Polzunkov appears to be a comic figure. He is physically unremarkable, socially awkward, and visibly nervous around others. His language is often jumbled, and he seems to lack the worldly poise of his colleagues. He is precisely the kind of figure that society designates as an easy target—someone whose presence is used to elevate others by comparison. Dostoevsky sets the story in a setting of superficial festivity: a party where laughter disguises cruelty and "camaraderie" cloaks condescension.

But the deeper irony, and indeed the tragedy, is that Polzunkov knows this. He is painfully aware that his invitation is not one of honor but of mockery. He senses that the host sees him as a curiosity, a clown to be displayed, and he endures the evening with stoic composure. It is this awareness, this silent endurance of public humiliation, that gives him moral weight. His behavior—awkward, trembling, and restrained—may appear comic to others, but within him is a profound emotional clarity. He understands what is happening to him. He suffers it. And still, he retains his composure.

Polzunkov's tragedy lies not in his weakness but in the indifference of those around him. He is not monstrous, corrupt, or mad—he is simply overlooked. And that, Dostoevsky suggests, may be the cruelest fate of all: to live among people who see you not as a fellow human being but as a source of entertainment or pity. Even those who might have defended him are afraid of social consequences. Thus, Polzunkov is not only laughed at but abandoned.

Yet within his resignation lies something noble. He does not lash out. He does not beg for approval. His restraint, though born of fear and shyness, becomes a kind of ethical stance—a quiet defiance. This moral thread, though subtle, is central to Dostoevsky's intention: the idea that the soul's dignity is not granted by others, but preserved in the face of their rejection. In Polzunkov's silent endurance, we glimpse a strength that the crowd cannot see.

This modern translation retains the tonal ambiguity—part pathos, part satire—of Dostoevsky's original while clarifying the emotional nuances for today's reader. The language has been updated for fluency and immediacy, ensuring that the narrative's psychological complexity and thematic subtlety are preserved.

In conclusion, Polzunkov is a quietly devastating story about the intersection of mockery and morality, spectacle and solitude. It confronts the reader with the everyday cruelty of social life and offers a meditation on the unseen strength of those who endure it. In a world that still elevates appearance over substance and laughter over empathy, Dostoevsky's little clerk remains a hero of quiet resistance—a reminder that true dignity often resides in those we least expect to possess it.

A Story

I began to study the man closely. There was something so strange about him that, no matter where my thoughts wandered, I couldn't help but fix my eyes on him and burst into uncontrollable laughter. That's exactly what happened to me. His eyes were so restless—or maybe he was so sensitive to the attention of others—that he seemed to instinctively know when someone was looking at him. The moment he felt watched, he would turn toward the observer and anxiously analyze their expression. His constant fidgeting and twisting made him look just like a dancing puppet. It was peculiar! He seemed terrified of being mocked, even though he practically made a living by acting as a clown for everyone and exposing himself to all sorts of ridicule—both moral and physical—based on the company he kept.

It's hard to pity someone who willingly plays the fool. Yet I quickly realized that this odd little man, as ridiculous as he appeared, wasn't a professional clown. There was still something gentlemanly about him. His uneasiness and constant self-consciousness actually spoke in his favor. I got the impression that his eagerness to please came more from a kind heart than from selfish motives. He allowed people to laugh loudly and inappropriately at him, right to his face. But I swear, his heart must have ached, knowing they weren't laughing at something he had done or said, but at him—his whole being, his personality, his appearance, his very existence.

I'm certain he felt the absurdity of his position, but any protest he might have had would die in his heart almost immediately—only to resurface again with surprising determination. I believe all of this stemmed from a kind heart, not from fear of being kicked out or of losing the chance to borrow money from someone. This man often borrowed money—in fact, that's how he survived. He asked for "loans" after entertaining people at his own expense, as though he'd earned the right to ask for help.

But what a sight it was when he asked! His small, wrinkled face could hold an astonishing variety of expressions, all at once. Shame, feigned boldness, frustration at his blushing, anger, fear of being rejected, desperation for forgiveness for daring to ask, a sense of his dignity, and an even greater sense of his humiliation—all these feelings flashed across his face like lightning. For six long years, he had struggled through life this way, never managing to approach the delicate act of borrowing money with ease or confidence. Despite everything, he never became hardened or entirely broken. His heart remained too sensitive, too passionate.

In my opinion, he was one of the most honest and decent men in the world, though he had one major flaw: he was willing to do anything—no matter how humiliating—just to help someone else, out of pure kindness and without expecting anything in return. In short, he was what people call "a pushover" in every sense of the word.

The most absurd part was that he dressed as well as anyone else, tidy and even slightly formal, as if trying to project an air of respectability. Yet this outward appearance clashed with his inner insecurity and constant self-deprecation, making him both laughable and pitiable at the same time. If, in his heart, he ever believed—even for a moment—that people were laughing out of good-natured amusement and not at his personal expense, I'm certain he would have willingly taken off his coat, worn it inside out, and walked around town that way—just to make others laugh and feel good.

But he could never truly feel equal to others. And here's another thing: he was proud, and even, in rare moments, brave. It was worth seeing how he could stand up to someone who had pushed him too far, confronting them with surprising boldness and almost heroic determination. But those moments didn't happen often. In essence, he was a martyr—one of the most useless and, therefore, one of the most comical martyrs imaginable.

A lively discussion was taking place among the guests. Suddenly, I noticed our peculiar friend leap onto his chair and shout at the top of his lungs, clearly eager to capture everyone's undivided attention.

"Listen," the host whispered to me, "he sometimes tells the most fascinating stories. Are you interested?"

I nodded and squeezed myself into the gathering crowd. The sight of a well-dressed man standing on a chair and yelling immediately grabbed everyone's attention. Those who didn't know him exchanged confused glances, while others burst into laughter.

"I knew Fedosey Nikolaitch. I probably knew Fedosey Nikolaitch better than anyone!" the peculiar man shouted from his elevated perch. "Gentlemen, let me tell you something. I know a great story about Fedosey Nikolaitch! A fantastic story!"

"Tell it, Osip Mihalitch, tell it!"

"Yes, tell us!"

"We're listening!"

"Listen, everyone!"

"I'll begin, but, gentlemen, this is quite a peculiar story..."

"Very good, go on!"

"It's a funny story."

"Excellent, let's hear it!"

"It's an incident from the private life of yours truly..."

"But why do you bother to announce that it's funny?" someone interrupted.

"And even a little tragic!" the man added dramatically.

"What??!" came the surprised reaction.

"In short," he said, waving his arms for emphasis, "this is a story that I believe you'll all enjoy hearing. Gentlemen, this story is the reason I've found myself in such distinguished and profitable company today..."

"No puns, please!" someone shouted.

"This story—"

"Get to the point! Finish the introduction!" another guest interjected impatiently.

"The story," a blond young man with a mustache said in a raspy voice, pulling a purse from his coat pocket as though by accident instead of a handkerchief, "the story, if it's worth hearing..."

"My dear sirs," the man on the chair continued, "this story is one that might make many of you wish to trade places with me. And finally," he added with a flourish, "this is the story of why I never got married."

"Married! A wife! Polzunkov trying to get married!"

"I admit, I'd like to meet Madame Polzunkov."

"May I ask the name of this supposed Madame Polzunkov?" a young man piped up, edging closer to the storyteller.

"Let's start with the first chapter, gentlemen. It was six years ago in the spring, March 31st—mark the date, gentlemen—on the eve..."

"Of April Fool's Day!" shouted a young man with curly hair.

"You catch on quickly. It was evening. Twilight was settling over the district town of N. The moon was just about to rise... everything perfectly timed. And so, during this very late twilight, I snuck out of my shabby lodging—after bidding farewell to my restricted grandmother, now departed. Forgive me, gentlemen, for using such a fashionable term, which I last heard from Nikolay Nikolaitch. But my grandmother truly was restricted: blind, mute, deaf, clueless—whatever you please. I confess I was nervous, ready for big things; my heart was racing like a kitten's when someone grabs it by the scruff of the neck."

"Excuse me, Monsieur Polzunkov," someone interrupted.

"What is it?"

"Could you tell it a bit more plainly? Don't overdo it, please."

"All right," said Osip Mihalitch, slightly thrown off. "I went into the house of Fedosey Nikolaitch—the house he had bought. You know, Fedosey Nikolaitch wasn't just some colleague; he was the full-fledged head of a department. I was announced and immediately shown into his study. I still remember it—the room was dim, almost dark, but they didn't bring any candles. Then Fedosey Nikolaitch walked in, and there we were, alone in the darkness."

"What happened next?" an officer asked.

"What do you think happened?" Polzunkov asked, turning quickly with a twitching expression to the young man with curls. "Well, gentlemen, something unusual

16

occurred—though really, it was nothing unusual. It's what you'd call an everyday matter. I simply took a roll of paper out of my pocket... and he took out a roll of paper too."

"Paper money?" someone guessed.

"Paper money. And we exchanged."

"I bet there's a whiff of bribery in this," remarked a well-dressed young man with short-cropped hair.

"Bribery?" Polzunkov repeated, almost shouting.

"'Oh, may I be a Liberal,

Such as many I have seen!'

If you, too, ever serve in the provinces, don't hesitate to warm your hands at your country's hearth. As an author once said, 'Even the smoke of our native land is sweet to us.' She's our Mother, gentlemen, our Mother Russia. We are her children, and so we suckle from her!"

The room erupted in laughter.

"Would you believe it, gentlemen, I have never taken a bribe?" Polzunkov said, glancing distrustfully around the room.

A loud, roaring wave of laughter drowned out his words.

"But it's true, gentlemen…"

He paused, his strange expression lingering as he looked around at everyone. Perhaps—who knows?— the thought struck him that he might be more honest than many in that respectable company. Either way, the seriousness in his face remained until the laughter subsided completely.

"And so," Polzunkov began again when it was quiet, "though I never took bribes, there was one time I made a mistake. I accepted a bribe… from someone who takes bribes. That is, I had certain documents in my possession that, if I had sent them to the right person, it would've gone badly for Fedosey Nikolaitch."

"So, he bought them from you?" someone asked.

"He did."

"Did he pay much?"

"He paid as much as some people today would sell their conscience for, completely, with all the extras—if they could get anything for it. But I felt like I was burning up when I put the money in my pocket. I can't explain it, gentlemen, but I was shaking all over. My lips were trembling, my legs felt weak. I was entirely to blame, fully guilty. I was so overcome with shame, I wanted to beg Fedosey Nikolaitch for forgiveness."

"And did he forgive you?"

"But I didn't ask for forgiveness… I only mean that's how I felt. You see, I have a sensitive heart. He looked me straight in the face and said, 'Osip Mihailitch, don't you fear God?' What could I do? Out of decency, I tilted my head to the side and raised my hands. 'In what way have I no fear of God, Fedosey Nikolaitch?' I asked, though I only said that to keep up appearances. Deep down, I wanted the ground to swallow me up. 'After being such a close friend to our family, practically like a son,' he said, 'and who knows what the future held for us, Osip Mihailitch? And now, suddenly, you're going to betray me? Tell me, how am I supposed to think of humanity after this?' He lectured me, gentlemen. 'Tell me,' he said again, 'what am I to think of mankind now, Osip Mihailitch?' What could he think? I had a lump in my throat, my voice was shaking, and, knowing my own miserable weakness, I grabbed my hat to leave.

'Where are you going, Osip Mihailitch?' he asked. 'Surely you don't hold a grudge against me on the eve of such a holy day? What wrong have I done to you?'

'Fedosey Nikolaitch,' I said, 'Fedosey Nikolaitch…' And that was it. I broke down, gentlemen. I melted like a sugar cube. And the roll of money in my pocket—it felt like it was screaming at me: 'You ungrateful wretch, you cursed thief!' It felt like it weighed a ton. If only it had weighed that much—it might have crushed me!

'You see,' said Fedosey Nikolaitch, 'I can see your regret. Tomorrow is…'

'St. Mary of Egypt's Day.'

'Well, don't cry,' he said, 'that's enough. You made a mistake, and you regret it! Come now! Maybe I can guide you back onto the right path.' He added, 'Perhaps my modest home will warm'—he hesitated, then said—'not your hardened, but your erring heart.' That's exactly what he said, I remember it clearly. Then he took me by the arm, gentlemen, and led me to his family circle. A cold shiver ran down my spine. I shuddered. I thought to myself, how could I face them? You must understand, gentlemen… what can I say? It was an awkward situation."

"Not Madame Polzunkov?" someone interrupted.

"Marya Fedosyevna—but she never had the chance, you see, to bear the name you've given her; she didn't achieve that honor. Fedosey Nikolaitch was right when he said I was almost like a son in their home. And it had been true, especially six months earlier when Mihailo Maximitch Dvigailov, a retired officer, was still alive.

But then, by God's will, he died, leaving everything unsettled until death sorted it out for him."

"Ugh!"

"Well, never mind, gentlemen, forgive me, that was a slip of the tongue. It's a bad pun, but the situation itself was far worse. I was left with no future ahead of me—except maybe a bullet through the brain. That officer, you see, though he never let me into his house (he lived well, always knew how to feather his nest), had believed—maybe rightly—that I was his son."

"Aha!"

"Yes, that's how it was. After that, things grew cold for me at Fedosey Nikolaitch's house. I noticed the change but kept quiet. Then, to make matters worse for me—or maybe better—a cavalry officer suddenly galloped into town, as unexpectedly as snow in April. His business—buying horses for the army—was brisk and lively, cavalry-style, but he made himself very comfortable at Fedosey Nikolaitch's, as though he were laying siege to the place!

"I approached the issue cautiously, as I tend to do. I asked what I'd done wrong, saying I'd always been like a son to him, and wondering when he might treat me like a father. Well, when he starts talking, you'd better settle in for an epic—a saga in twelve cantos! He'll go on and on, and you're left nodding, licking your lips, throwing up your hands in confusion. Not a single shred of sense comes through. He fogs you up completely, wriggling like an eel, slipping through your grasp. It's a real talent—a gift, you could say—and even if it doesn't affect you directly, it's still unnerving.

"I tried everything, went this way and that. I brought songs to the lady of the house, gave her sweets, came up with clever things to say. I sighed, groaned, and poured out my heart. 'My chest hurts,' I told her, 'hurts from love.' I even resorted to tears and secret declarations. What a fool I was! Never mind that I was thirty—didn't cross my mind! I used every trick in the book. It was no use. I got nothing but mockery and ridicule in return.

"I was furious, humiliated. I stopped going to the house. I thought and thought, and finally, in my anger, I decided to betray him. Yes, it was a vile thing to do—I admit that. But I had plenty of evidence, solid evidence—a case that was worth its weight in gold. It fetched me fifteen hundred roubles when I traded it in for cash!"

"Ah, so that was the bribe?"

"Yes, sir, that was the bribe. And it was taken from a bribe-taker, so I didn't do anything wrong—I swear it!

Now let me continue. Fedosey Nikolaitch dragged me—more dead than alive—into the room where they were having tea. Everyone greeted me like I'd deeply offended them. Not exactly offended, though—more like hurt, deeply hurt, as if they were shattered by my actions. At the same time, they all wore expressions of dignity, solemnity, almost parental concern, as though welcoming back a prodigal son.

"They made me sit down for tea, though I didn't need any. I already felt like a boiling samovar was burning in my chest, and my feet were blocks of ice. I was humbled, completely cowed. Marya Fominishna, his wife, spoke to me warmly, almost motherly, right from the start.

"'Why have you gotten so thin, my dear boy?' she asked.

"'I haven't been well, Marya Fominishna,' I replied, though my voice trembled miserably."

"And then, all of a sudden—she must have been waiting for the chance to take a jab at me, that old snake—she said:

"'I suppose your conscience got the better of you, Osip Mihalitch, my dear! Our fatherly hospitality must have weighed on you! You've been punished for the tears I've shed.'

"Yes, she actually said that! She had the nerve to come out with it. That was nothing to her, though—she was a terror! She just sat there pouring tea, but if she were in the marketplace, I swear she'd outshout any fishwife. That's the kind of woman she was.

"And then, to my misfortune, the daughter, Marya Fedosyevna, walked in. She was so innocent-looking, a little pale, and her eyes were red like she'd been crying. I was floored on the spot like a fool. But, as it turned out, those tears were for the cavalry officer. He had left town for good—packed up and gone. And it was about time, too! I might as well mention it now; it wasn't that his leave had expired exactly, but… well, you know. It was only later that her loving parents put two and two together and figured out what had happened. What could they do? They kept the whole thing quiet—an addition to the family!

"I couldn't help myself—as soon as I looked at her, I was done for. I stole a glance at my hat, thinking I might make a quick escape. But they took my hat away, of course. I even thought about sneaking out without it, but then they locked the doors.

"There were friendly jokes, winks, little graces. I was embarrassed out of my mind. I said something stupid, talked nonsense about love. Then my charmer sat down

24

at the piano and, with a look of wounded pride, sang that song about the hussar leaning on his sword. That finished me off completely.

"'Well,' said Fedosey Nikolaitch, 'all is forgiven—come to my arms!'

"I fell right into him, my face buried in his waistcoat.

"'My benefactor! You're a father to me!' I cried, shedding a flood of hot tears. Lord have mercy, what a scene it was! He cried, his good wife cried, Mashenka cried, and even some blonde little thing there started crying too.

"That wasn't enough—then the younger children crept out from every corner (the Lord had truly filled their quiver!) and started wailing as well. Such tears, such emotion, such joy! It was like a prodigal son coming home, or a soldier returning to his family.

"Afterward, there were refreshments. We played forfeits and games. 'I have a pain.' 'Where is it?' 'In my heart.' 'Who gave it to you?' My charmer blushed, and I was completely won over. The old man and I had some punch, and that was it—they had me.

"I went back to my grandmother in a daze, laughing all the way home. For two full hours, I paced up and down our little room, still dizzy from it all. I woke up my poor granny and told her about my happiness.

"'But did he give you any money, that brigand?' she asked.

"'He did, Granny, he did, my dear! Luck has come pouring in—so much that all we have to do is open our hands to catch it.'

"I even woke up Sofron.

"'Sofron,' I said, 'take off my boots.'

"Sofron pulled them off, and I grabbed his hands.

"'Come on, Sofron, congratulate me! Give me a kiss! I'm going to get married, my boy—married! Tomorrow, you can get drunk if you want, have a spree, my dear fellow—your master is getting married!'"

"My heart was full of jokes and laughter. I was about to drift off to sleep, but something made me get up again. I sat and thought: tomorrow is the first of April, a bright and playful day—what could I do? And then an idea struck me. Gentlemen, I got out of bed, lit a candle, and sat down at the writing table just as I was. I was so excited, completely carried away. Do you know what it feels like when you're completely carried away? I joyfully indulged in my foolishness, my dear friends.

"You see, this is the kind of person I am: someone takes something from me, and instead of holding back, I give them something else too and say, 'Here, take this as well.' They slap me on the cheek, and in my joy, I turn and offer them my back. They try to lure me like a dog with a treat, and I throw myself at them, paws out, kissing them with all my heart. Just look at what I'm doing now, gentlemen! You're laughing, whispering—I can see it! After I finish my story, you'll mock me, you'll attack me, but still, I keep talking, talking, talking! Who tells me to do this? Who pushes me to it? Who stands behind me whispering, 'Speak, speak and tell them'? And yet I keep talking, trying to please you, as though you're my brothers, my dearest friends… Oh!"

The laughter that had started slowly now completely drowned out the speaker's voice, though he seemed to be in a kind of trance. He stopped, looked around at the group for several minutes, then suddenly, as if caught in a whirlwind, waved his hand, burst out laughing himself, as though he truly found his own position ridiculous, and began his story again.

"I hardly slept that night, gentlemen. I spent it scribbling away, you see—I had thought of a prank. Ah, even remembering it now, I'm ashamed. It wouldn't have been so bad if it had all happened during the night. Maybe I could have blamed it on being drunk, or just making a mistake, or rambling nonsense. But no! I woke up in the morning as soon as it got light. I'd only slept an hour or two, and yet I was still determined.

"I got dressed, washed up, pomaded and curled my hair, put on my new dress coat, and headed straight to spend the holiday with Fedosey Nikolaitch. And I kept the joke I'd written in my hat.

"He welcomed me again with open arms, inviting me into his fatherly embrace. But I struck a serious pose. I had my prank ready in my mind. I took a step back.

"'No, Fedosey Nikolaitch,' I said, 'but will you please read this letter,' and I handed it to him along with my daily report. And do you know what was in that letter? It said, 'For such-and-such reasons, the aforementioned Osip Mihalitch requests to be discharged.' And under my petition, I signed with my full rank. Can you believe it? What an idea! My God, it was the cleverest thing I could come up with!

"Since it was April Fool's Day, I wanted to pretend that I was still upset, that I'd changed my mind overnight, and was more offended than ever. It was like I was saying, 'My dear benefactor, I don't want to know you or your daughter anymore. I pocketed the money yesterday, so I'm secure. Here's my resignation, requesting to leave this office. I don't want to work under someone like Fedosey Nikolaitch anymore. I'll find another job—and maybe I'll even report you.'

"I was pretending to be a complete scoundrel, hoping to frighten them. What a way to scare them, right? A fine idea, wasn't it? You see, my heart had softened toward them since the day before, so I thought I'd have a little fun with the family. I wanted to tease the fatherly heart of Fedosey Nikolaitch.

"As soon as he took my letter and opened it, I saw his entire expression change."

"'What's the meaning of this, Osip Mihalitch?' he asked.

"And like a fool, I replied, 'The first of April! Many happy returns of the day, Fedosey Nikolaitch!'—just like some silly schoolboy hiding behind his grandmother's chair and shouting 'Boo!' to scare her. Yes... yes, I feel so ashamed even talking about it, gentlemen! No, I won't tell you."

"Nonsense! What happened then?" someone asked.

"Come on, tell us! Yes, go on," voices encouraged me from all sides.

"There was such an uproar and commotion, my dear friends! Exclamations of surprise everywhere! 'You naughty man, you mischievous fellow,' they said, all so sweetly that I felt ashamed. I wondered how someone like me, such a sinner, could even step into a home as virtuous as theirs.

"'Well, my dear boy,' said the mother, 'you gave me such a fright that my legs are still trembling! I can hardly stand! I rushed to Masha as if I'd gone mad: "Mashenka," I said, "what will become of us? See how your friend turned out!" And, my dear boy, I misjudged you. Forgive an old woman like me; I was mistaken! I thought maybe last night, after you got home late, you started imagining things, thinking we invited you over on purpose to... to trap you. I was so upset at the thought! Stop it, Mashenka, don't wink at me like that! Osip Mihalitch isn't a stranger! I'm your mother. I wouldn't speak ill of you! Thank God, I'm not twenty anymore—I'm forty-five!"'

"Gentlemen, I nearly threw myself at her feet on the spot. Once again, there were tears, and there were kisses. Then the jokes began. Even Fedosey Nikolaitch decided to join in, claiming some magical fiery bird flew in with a letter in its diamond beak! He was trying to fool us too—oh, how we laughed! How touched we all were! Honestly, I feel embarrassed even talking about it.

"So, my dear friends, here's how it ended: one day passed, then two, then three—a week went by, and I was officially engaged to her. Of course, I was! The wedding rings were ordered, and the date was set. They just didn't want to announce it publicly until the Inspector's visit was over. I was counting the days until his arrival because my happiness depended on it. I couldn't wait for him to finish so we could move forward.

"In the meantime, amidst all the excitement, Fedosey Nikolaitch dumped all the work on me—balancing the accounts, writing reports, checking the books. Everything was a complete mess—disorder everywhere! Still, I thought, 'I need to help my future father-in-law.' But he started falling ill. His health seemed to worsen every day. And I, gentlemen, became so thin I could've snapped like a twig. I was terrified I might collapse. But I managed to finish everything and get his affairs in order.

"Then, one day, a messenger came for me. I rushed over in a panic, wondering what could've happened. I found Fedosey Nikolaitch with his head wrapped in a vinegar compress, frowning, sighing, and groaning.

"'My dear boy, my son,' he said, 'if I die, who will take care of you all, my darlings?'

"His wife trailed in behind him with all their children; Mashenka was crying, and I started blubbering too.

"'Oh no,' he said, 'God will be merciful. He won't punish you for my sins.'

"Then he sent them all out of the room, told me to shut the door behind them, and we were left alone, just the two of us.

"'I have a favor to ask of you,' he said."

"'What kind of favor?' I asked.

"'Oh, my dear boy, even on my deathbed, there's no peace for me. I'm in need.'

"'In need? How?' I felt myself flush with embarrassment and could barely speak.

"'You see, I had to use some of my own money to cover Treasury expenses. I don't mind sacrificing for the greater good, my boy—I'd give my very life. Don't think anything bad of me. It pains me that slanderers have tarnished my name in your eyes. You misunderstood. My hair has turned gray from sorrow. The Inspector is on his way, and Matveyev is short seven thousand rubles. I'll have to take the blame for it. Who else? It will all fall on me, my boy. They'll ask where my oversight was. And how can we get the money from Matveyev? The man's had enough trouble already. Why should I ruin him further?'

"'My goodness,' I thought. 'What a fair and noble man! What a heart he has!'

"'And I don't want to touch my daughter's dowry. That money is sacred. Yes, I have my own funds, but they're all tied up in loans to friends—how can I gather them up in a moment?'

"I couldn't help myself. I dropped to my knees before him. 'My benefactor!' I cried, 'I've wronged you, I've misjudged you. Slanderers spoke against you. Please, don't break my heart. Take your money back!'

"He looked at me with tears in his eyes. 'That's exactly what I expected from you, my son. Stand up! I forgave you long ago, for my daughter's sake. Now, my heart forgives you completely. You've healed my wounds. I bless you for all time!'

"When he blessed me, gentlemen, I hurried home as fast as I could. I gathered the money and returned to him.

"'Here it is, Father,' I said. 'I've only spent fifty rubles.'

"'That's fine,' he replied. 'But now, every little bit matters. Time is short. Write a report, backdated a few days, explaining that you borrowed fifty rubles in advance because you were short. I'll inform the authorities it was approved in advance.'

"And, gentlemen, can you believe it? I wrote that report too!"

"And then? What happened after that? How did it end?"

"As soon as I handed over the report, this is how it ended. The next morning, a government envelope arrived. I opened it, and what do you think it was? A dismissal notice! I was ordered to hand over my work, deliver the accounts, and leave my post!"

"'How could this be?' I cried.

"'Exactly,' I shouted at the top of my lungs, 'How could this be?' My ears were ringing, but I couldn't understand why. Then it hit me—the Inspector had arrived in town. My heart sank. 'This is no coincidence,' I thought. And just like that, I rushed over to Fedosey Nikolaitch.

"'What's going on here?' I asked.

"'What do you mean?' he replied.

"'I've been dismissed.'

"'Dismissed? How?'

"'Just look at this!' I said, shoving the notice at him."

"'Well, what about it?' he asked."

"'But I didn't ask for this!' I replied."

"'Oh, but you did. You submitted your resignation on the first of April.' (I had never taken back that letter!)"

"'Fedosey Nikolaitch! I can't believe this. I can't believe it's you!'"

"'Yes, it's me. Why?'"

"'My God!'"

"'I'm sorry, sir. I'm really sorry that you decided to leave the service so soon. A young man should stay in the service, but you've started to lose your focus lately. As for your record, don't worry—I'll take care of that. Your behavior has always been excellent.'"

"'But that letter was just a joke, Fedosey Nikolaitch! I didn't mean it. I only gave it to you as part of a fatherly ... gesture, that's all.'"

"'That's all? A strange kind of joke, sir. Do you think one jokes with official documents like that? People get sent to Siberia for less! Well, goodbye. I'm busy. The Inspector is here, and duty comes first. You can enjoy your freedom, but we have work to do. Oh, and I'll write you a recommendation. One more thing—I've" just bought Matveyev's house. We're moving in a day or two, so I doubt we'll have the pleasure of seeing you at our new home. Bon voyage!'

"I ran home.

"'We're ruined, Granny!' I cried.

"She wailed, poor woman, and then I saw a page from Fedosey Nikolaitch running up with a note and a birdcage. Inside the cage was a starling. In a moment of kindness, I had given her that starling. The note simply said, 'April 1st,' and nothing else. What do you think of that, gentlemen?"

"'And then what? What happened next?' they asked.

"'What then? I ran into Fedosey Nikolaitch again, intending to call him a scoundrel to his face.'

"'Well, did you?'

"'No, somehow I just couldn't bring myself to do it, gentlemen.'"

Thank You for Reading

Dear Reader,

We hope this timeless classic has sparked your imagination and enriched your literary journey. Now that you've turned the final page, we want to share a vision for the future of reading—one where every classic you've ever wanted to explore is at your fingertips, in a format that best suits your life.

We'd like to invite you to gain immediate, unlimited digital & audiobook access to hundreds of the most treasured literary classics ever written—along with the option to secure deluxe paperback, hardcover & box set editions at printing cost. Together, we can spark a new global literary renaissance alongside our small, independent publishing house called "The Library of Alexandria."

Thousands of years ago, the Library of Alexandria stood as a beacon of knowledge—until it was lost to history. We aim to reignite that spirit of preservation and discovery right now, in the modern age—only this time, it's accessible to all, in every language and every format.

Picture a world where every timeless classic, novel, poem, or philosophical treatise is not only available to read but also updated for today's readers—modernized, translated into any language or dialect, and ready to enjoy in any format you choose, whether that is in an eBook, audiobook, paperback, or deluxe hardcover & box set version a printing cost.

By joining our movement to rebuild the modern Library of Alexandria, you become part of an unprecedented mission to offer:

Unlimited Audiobook & eBook Access to the Greatest Classics of All Time

Instantly explore thousands of legendary works, from Plato and Shakespeare to Jane Austen and Leo Tolstoy. All are instantly ready to read or listen to, giving you a complete literary universe at your fingertips.

Paperback & Deluxe Editions at Printing Costs:

Purchase any title in a paperback, deluxe hardbound, or deluxe boxset edition at printing costs, shipped right to your doorstep. Curate your personal library of Alexandria with editions worthy of display— crafted to last, designed to captivate, and delivered straight to your door.

Modern translations for Contemporary Readers in all languages and dialects

Discover a vast selection of classics reimagined in clear, current language—no more struggling with outdated phrases or obscure references. Next to the original versions, we aim to offer translations in as many languages and dialects as possible.

As we continue our translation efforts and add new languages, readers everywhere can connect with these works as if they were written today. By bridging linguistic divides, you're contributing to ensuring that these timeless stories become more meaningful, accessible, and inspiring for people across the globe.

Your Personal Library of Alexandria:

Over the months and years, you'll curate a unique physical archive of classics—each volume a testament to your taste, curiosity, and love of knowledge. It's not just about owning books—it's about curating a cultural legacy you'll cherish and pass down for generations to come.

Join a Global Literary Renaissance:

Your support fuels an ongoing mission: allowing us to reinvest in offering deluxe print editions (including special boxsets) at their true cost, broaden the range of available formats and translations, and extend the reach of these works to new audiences worldwide. By joining today, you're not just preserving a legacy of masterpieces; you set in motion a powerful wave of literary accessibility.

We are more than a publisher—we're a movement, and we can't do it alone. Your support lets us scale our mission, preserving and reimagining history's greatest works for tomorrow's readers.

Become a Torchbearer of knowledge.

Thank you for picking up this book and allowing us into your literary journey. As you turn the pages, know that you're part of something larger: a global effort to keep these stories alive, share their wisdom across borders and generations, and spark a true cultural revival for the modern era.

If this resonates with you—please consider taking the next step by visiting:

www.libraryofalexandria.com

With gratitude and a shared love of knowledge,

The Modern Library of Alexandria Team

Visit:

www.libraryofalexandria.com

Or scan the code below:

9 7 8 1 8 0 4 2 1 9 0 8 9